# Slugs in Love

by
Susan Pearson

illustrated by
Kevin O'Malley

Herbie    Marylou

SCHOLASTIC INC.
New York  Toronto  London  Auckland  Sydney
Mexico City  New Delhi  Hong Kong  Buenos Aires

ISBN-13: 978-0-545-06065-3
ISBN-10: 0-545-06065-6

20 19 18 17 16 15 14                    19 20 21 22/0

Printed in the U.S.A.          40

First Scholastic printing, January 2008

The text of this book is set in Garamond.

The illustrations were created using markers,
colored pencils, and Photoshop.

Book design by Symon Chow

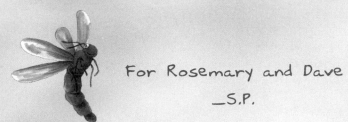

For Rosemary and Dave
—S.P.

arylou loved everything about Herbie—how his slime trail glistened in the dark, how he could stretch himself thin to squeeze inside the cellar window, how he always found the juiciest tomato. Though she never spoke a single word to him—she was too shy—she thought about Herbie every morning and every night and most of the hours in between.

On Monday, while she grazed in the strawberry patch, Herbie filled her mind and a love poem filled her heart. She wrote it in slime on the watering can.

Strawberries are red.
Blueberries are blue.
Herbie is handsome.
Love,
Marylou

The next morning, Herbie found it. He looked around. There were already at least sixty slugs in the garden. Which one, he wondered, was Marylou?

Herbie decided to send a message back. He wrote it on the garden hoe.

Marylou, which one are you?
Meet me here at half past two,
Yours truly,
Herbie

-BURPEE-
-forget-me-
nots

But the gardener put the hoe
away in the barn, so Marylou never
saw Herbie's message.

On Tuesday, while Marylou was hiding from the sun in the ivy, she saw Herbie hiding under a stone, and a poem came immediately to mind. She wrote it on the wheelbarrow later that day.

The sun is shining all around.
It shines on field and tree.
But Herbie's safe beneath a rock—
I wish he'd think of me.
                    Love,
                    Marylou

"Marylou loves Herrrrrrbie!" teased Jethro on Wednesday morning.

Herbie blushed. "Who *is* Marylou?" he asked, but Jethro didn't know either.

Herbie sent another message. This time he wrote it on a
fence where it would stay put.

To Marylou:
You could make my life complete!
I'd love to meet someone so sweet.
Tell me where and I'll be there.
Sincerely,
Herbie

But that afternoon it rained and his letter washed away.

Even when Marylou was sleeping, poems to Herbie filled her dreams. She woke early and wrote another poem on the scarecrow.

"That Marylou is some poet!" said Sammy.

"Do you know her?" Herbie asked excitedly.

"I think she's the brownish one," said Sammy.

All day long Herbie searched for a brownish
slug, but next to the brown dirt, they all looked
a little brown. Herbie left another
message on the watermelons.

Your poems make me happy.
Your poems make me glad.
But I can't find you, Marylou,
and that makes me feel sad!
Your friend,

Herbie

But Marylou was in the squash patch
that day and didn't see Herbie's note. She
left another poem behind on the zucchini.

Herbie was at his wit's end. He *had* been noticing her! Well, her poems anyway. And he'd asked everyone he could think of if they knew her.

"I think she's the greenish one," said Homer.

"I think she's the pinkish one," said Jodelle.

"Maybe she's the one who likes tomatoes," said Adelaide.

"*All* slugs like tomatoes!" said Herbie.

But Adelaide had given him an idea.

Herbie climbed to the
top of the tallest tomato
plant. On his way back
down, he wrote a message.

And that night, when Marylou went
out to snack on a tomato, she found
Herbie's message glistening in the
garden! What joy! What gladness!
What delight! Marylou could
hardly contain herself as she
hurried to the barn.

The next morning, the first thing Herbie saw was:

As always, when she saw Herbie, poetry filled
Marylou's head. She said:

"Herbie, I am Marylou.

We meet at last. How do you do?"

Herbie was tongue-tied. Suddenly he felt shy.
But at last he blurted out:

"I am fine.

Will you be mine?"

Marylou and Herbie
lived happily ever after.